To:

_____

From:

_____

Date:

_____

God Bless You & GOOD NIGHT

Written by Hannah C. Hall

Illustrated by Steve Whitlow

An Imprint of Thomas Nelson

Published in Nashville, Tennessee, by Tommy Nelson. Tommy Nelson is an imprint of Thomas Nelson. Thomas Nelson is a registered trademark of HarperCollins Christian Publishing, Inc.

Tommy Nelson titles may be purchased in bulk for educational, business, fund-raising, or sales promotional use. For information, please e-mail SpecialMarkets@ThomasNelson.com.

Scripture quotations are taken from the International Children's Bible®. Copyright © 1986, 1988, 1999, 2015 by Thomas Nelson. Used by permission. All rights reserved.

ISBN: 978-1-4003-0897-2

Library of Congress Cataloging-in-Publication Data
Names: Hall, Hannah C., author. | Whitlow, Steve, illustrator.
Title: God bless you & good night / written by Hannah C. Hall ; illustrated
  by Steve Whitlow.
Other titles: God bless you and good night
Description: Nashville, Tennessee : Thomas Nelson, 2018. | Summary:
  Illustrations and short rhymes follow animal families as they go through
  bedtime routines, such as having a snack or getting a favorite blanket or
  toy.
Identifiers: LCCN 2017021872 | ISBN 9781400308972 (hardback)
Subjects: | CYAC: Stories in rhyme. | Bedtime--Fiction. | Animals--Fiction.
Classification: LCC PZ8.3.H1443 Go 2018 | DDC [E]--dc23 LC record available at
https://lccn.loc.gov/2017021872

Printed in China
18 19 20 21 22 DSC 6 5 4 3 2 1

Mfr: DSC / Shenzhen, China / January 2018 / PO #9459667

The Lord gives sleep to those he loves.

—Psalm 127:2

It's time to stretch from small to tall
To see the moon so bright.
It lights our way and seems to say,
"God bless you and good night."

Was that a little growl I heard?
It sounded like your tummy.
Let's get a snack then hit the sack.
You're needing something yummy!

Who's ready for a bedtime bath?
The bubbles reach the sky!
I filled the tub, so scrub-a-dub,
And watch those bubbles fly!

Now get yourself all dressed for bed.
Your jammies make me giggle.
You're oh-so-sweet from head to feet—
Those flippers really wiggle!

Come climb up here on Mama's lap
And read a book with me.
I know of one that's lots of fun.
Hop over and you'll see!

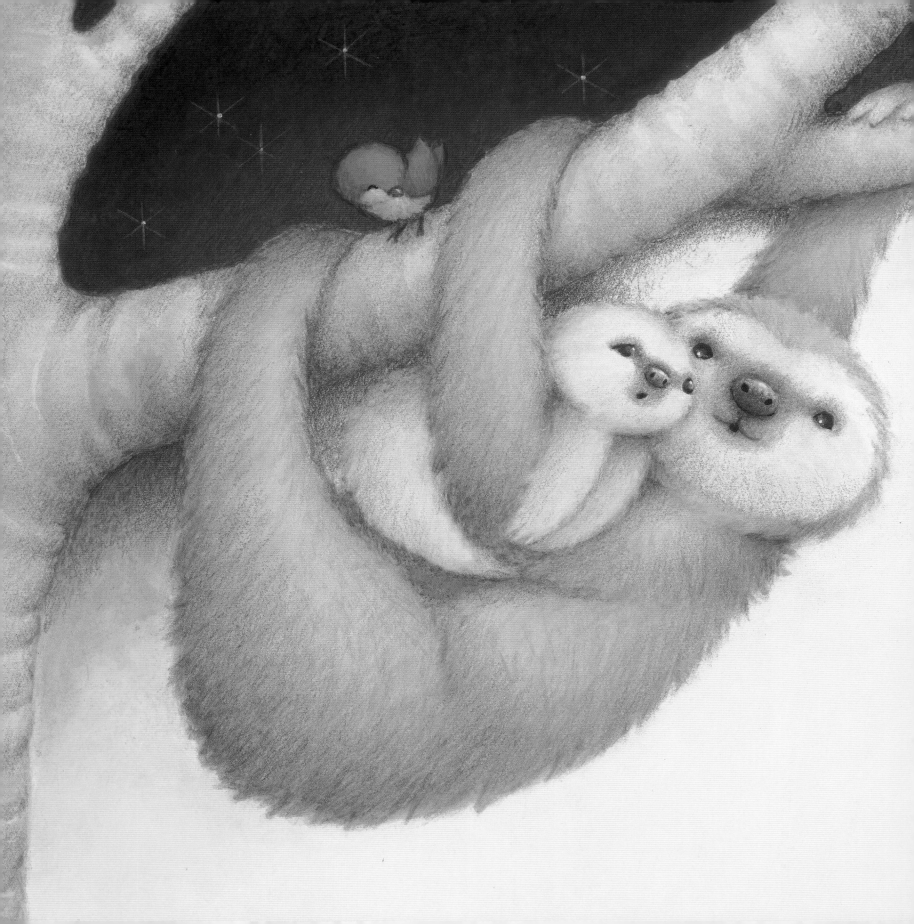

We'll find a comfy place to sleep.

Let's go even higher!

Climbing trees is such a breeze,

But, **yaaaawn**, I sure am tired.

We count our blessings every night—
God gives us gifts each day!
Today is done. The moon has come.
It's time to hit the hay.

I'll wrap you safely in my arms
And squeeze my snuggle bug.
There's nothing more that I adore
Than a sleepy bedtime hug.

Let's settle down and settle in
And close our eyes to pray.
You've wrestled, raced, and run and chased.
"God, thank You for this day."

It's time to sing a lullaby.
Who, who should choose the song?
There's one I love 'bout God above,
And you can sing along.

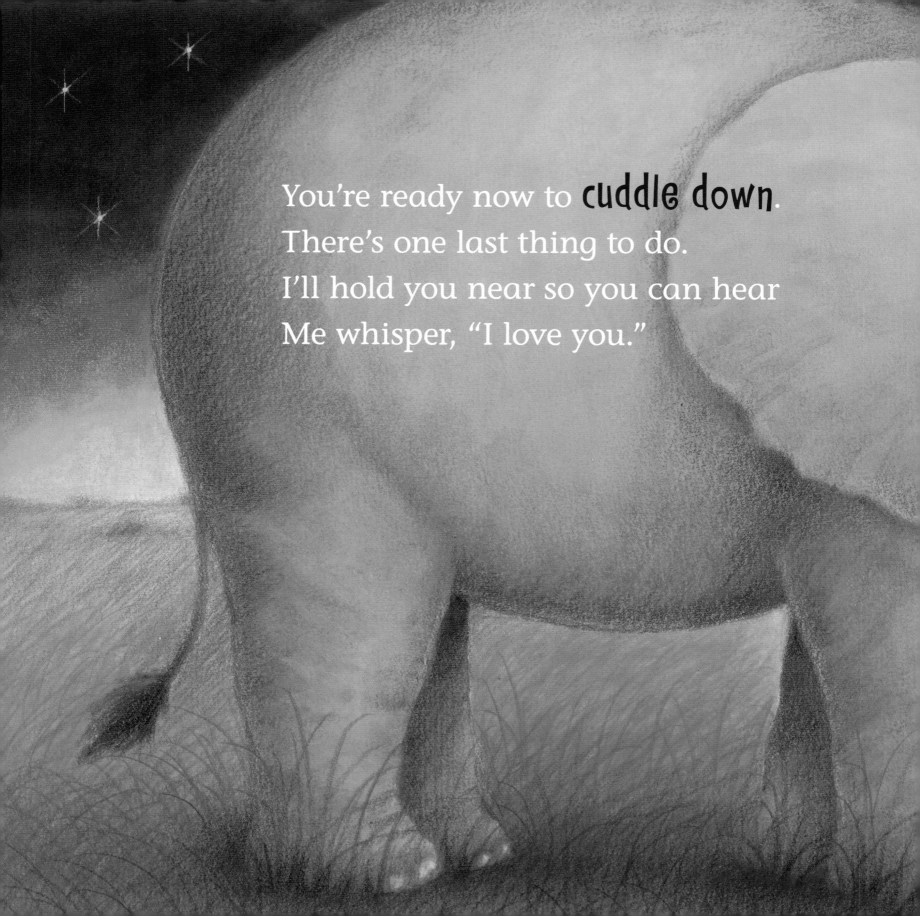

You're ready now to cuddle down.
There's one last thing to do.
I'll hold you near so you can hear
Me whisper, "I love you."

Be sure to grab your teddy bear
And snuggly blanket too.
Now count your sheep; don't make a peep.
Sweet sleep will come to you!

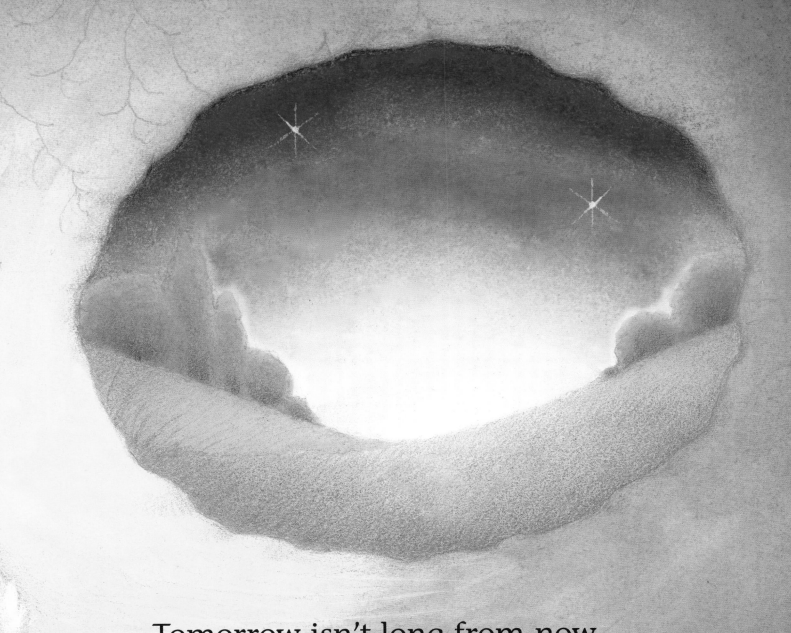

Tomorrow isn't long from now.
It's just a night away.
So close your eyes; don't be surprised
When tomorrow is today!

The night-light's glowing just enough.
You're tucked in toasty tight.
It's time for bed, you fuzzy head.
God bless you and good night.